THIS COLORING BOOK BELONGS TO:

_____

Hey there! I'm Sunflo, and I'm thrilled you snagged my cozy season coloring book! It's part of my bold and easy series, packed with delightful designs just waiting to whisk you into relaxation mode. Be sure to check out my other creations too! Enjoy the cozy vibes!

Cozy Season Checklist

- ☺ Pumpkin Apron
- ☺ Pumpkin Pie
- ☺ Teddy Bear Teapot
- ☺ Candy-Corn Lipgloss
- ☺ Apple Slippers
- ☺ Cozy Robe
- ☺ Pug in a Mug
- ☺ Teddy Bear Socks
- ☺ Seasonal Pictures
- ☺ Apple Cider

- ☺ Incense Oil Diffuser
- ☺ Beanie Hat
- ☺ Rocking Chair
- ☺ Pumpkin Bracelet
- ☺ Seasonal Drinks
- ☺ Ghost Sugar Cookies
- ☺ Cinnamon Roll Candle
- ☺ Leaf Sweater
- ☺ Cozy Boots
- ☺ Pumpkin Teddy Bear

Cozy Season Checklist Pg. 2

ʊ Patchwork Blanket
ʊ Ghost Phone Case
ʊ Moon Mug
ʊ S'mores Tissue Box
ʊ Honey Jar
ʊ Ghost Strawberry
ʊ Bobbing for Apples
ʊ Pumpkin Sheet Masks
ʊ Pumpkin Alarm Clock
ʊ Simmer Pot

ʊ Pumpkin Bathtub
ʊ Stack of Books
ʊ Candy-Corn Nail Polish
ʊ Cozy Animal Hoodie
ʊ Pumpkin on a Pillow
ʊ Ghost Boba Tea
ʊ Comfort Cake
ʊ Ghost Plant
ʊ Cozy Kitten
ʊ Acorn Mittens

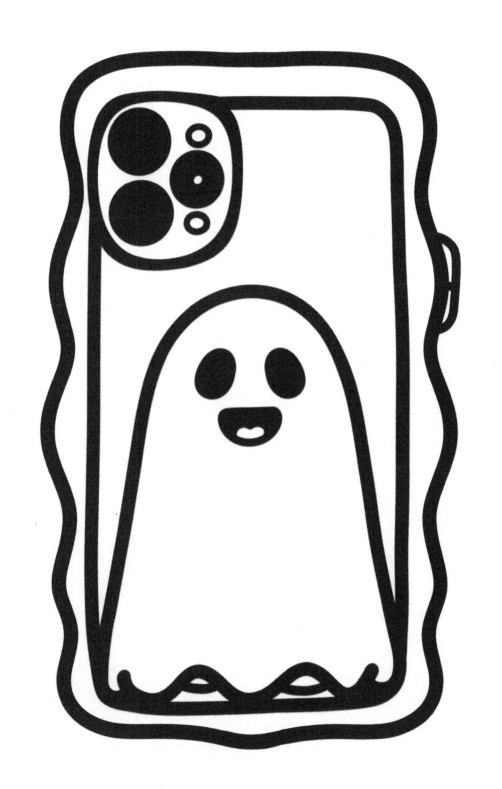

Made in United States
North Haven, CT
16 November 2024

60432139R00050